VIVI'S WAR

Marie-Antoinette Alpert

Arkus Books

First published in the United States in 2018 by

Arkus Books

For information, contact:

Arkus

CES Publishing

2701 Shasta Rd

Berkeley, CA 94708

Services@patternlanguage.com

Library of Congress Cataloging-in-Publication Date

is available from publisher upon request

Jacket design and book composition by Lucky Bard Enterprises.

Cover illustration by Jean-Marie (Mény) Robert.

First Edition

paperback ISBN: 978-1-732330-60-3

For those who survived, and those who did not.

Table of Contents

Author's Note

I'm old now, but I can see my young mother more clearly than ever, bouncing me blissfully on her strong legs, prancing and laughing through the woods and enchanted vales of Brittany — an ageless being from another time. Because I lost her at such a vulnerable age, part of me has remained a precocious five-and-a-half year old — too tall for her years — struggling to blend in with the world of adults but never quite able to compose with the complexities and the necessary concessions of adult life.

I wrote *Vivi's War* so that my own child, born a galaxy away in America, could discover an important chapter of his family history, and gain some insights into those desperate times. Ours was a family torn asunder by war, but we were also a rather typical French family, forced to make countless concessions to survive, and forced to become something other than what we had been: a clan of renowned naval officers, artists, and political reformers. We were brought down by the war, and eventually destroyed. My sisters and myself survived the ordeal, but at what cost? My greatest hope is that *Vivi's War* will help grownups glimpse the secret world of children, who must grapple with tragedy and loss in ways that are typically lost on their parents and guides. Vivi inhabits this hidden universe, this churning realm of wonder and sorrow.

--Belle-Ile-en-Mer, July 2018

Chapter One

This morning the doctor's wife took us back home. And the first thing I noticed was that the vases full of yellow primroses were all gone. We had picked them in the woods with Maman the afternoon before our baby brother got lost and became an angel. Maman sat at the foot of a big oak, inside the great roots. She smiled, "It is almost spring; children, dance, dance!" And I swirled like a top and danced around the tree. She laughed, "You little sprout, bouncing on wire legs, I'll catch you, wait, I'll catch you..." Each time I reappeared by her side, she gave me a squeeze. I squealed, running to the other side of the tree as fast as I could, until she called out to me.

"I'll find you Vivi. Wherever you hide."

But she could hardly get up from the twisted roots; we had piled primroses on her legs until they were all covered up. When Claire, who is just an annoying baby, climbed on her and started throwing the flowers all over the place, Maman laughed, hugging her again and again, calling her "my sweet lamb."

When we returned home that afternoon, there weren't even enough vases in the house for all our primroses. We had to use the kitchen glasses. It took us a long time to arrange the tiny pink stems and place the vases everywhere, even in our father's room. As we climbed the stairs that evening to go to bed, Maman had said, "The house smells of spring."

Now it smells of nothing. The first thing Mémé told us this morning is that we are not to enter Maman's room. All the time we were at the doctor's house I wanted to go back home to check if Maman had come back, because even though they thought I could not hear them, I listened to the people

9

speaking about her. "Those poor children. Yes, what a way to go, and only the day before she was in the woods. Maybe it was the damp ground she sat on." Even the washerwoman, who never smiles and works all winter long at the spring, her hands purple and cracked with blisters, was talking about it. "Just the thought of it. I could cry."

Maman was asleep when we went to her room that evening. Now, Mémé tells us that our baby brother flew up to Limbo, to become an angel. Yet, people say that he is lost, like Maman. Where is Limbo? And where did Maman get lost? Mémé won't answer me when I ask her again and again. Finally, she turned to me and almost yelled "in Pa-ra-dise!" And she spilled half her plate of soup on the kitchen table. When she cleaned up the soup she kept repeating "sapristi-sapristi," her favorite word when she's angry. So that I didn't dare ask her what "Paradise" meant. "Sapristi" almost sounds like "sacristy," the priest's room at the church where no one enters. But "sapristi" doesn't means anything.

Mémé often uses words that don't mean anything, and "Paradise" is one of them.

No one sleeps in Maman's room anymore. Our beds have been moved into Mémé's room. For a moment I entered Maman's room. It must be true what they say about Maman being lost because her room is cold and empty. Even the crib is gone. The mattress on her gold and black bed is as flat as the beach road. They've placed an old rug with tiny brown flowers on it, and they've taken away all the pillows and blankets. Our neighbor, Madame Corentin, and Thérèse, who comes to help every day, have scrubbed the floor clean underneath Maman's high bed, but they couldn't clean the mattress.

"Too blood-stained," I heard them tell Mémé.

Was Maman hurt before she got lost?

When I hurt my fingers some time ago, I saw the blood pour out, and it melted into Maman's bathrobe as she carried me, running to the doctor's house. And I turned my head the other way in the doctor's office when he said I shouldn't look as he cut the dangling tips. I fell asleep for a long time and I woke up, almost cured, in Maman's bed.

Chapter Two

The last time we saw Maman she had been lying on her side on top of her bed. She was wearing the wine-red bathrobe she only wore in the morning. But it was evening, the yellow velvet curtains had been drawn shut for the night.

No one spoke in her room as we entered it. And I hardly could hear when Mémé whispered "Come now, come over here. Say goodbye," because her voice had crumbled like a sand castle when a wave runs over it. She led all four of us to the far dark end of the room. "Come, come see your baby brother." And once again her voice had crumbled away.

He lay very small on top of Maman's desk, his lace dress reaching all the way to the floor. It felt cold in that corner of the room. His tiny hands on his chest were the color of the dress. Mémé said, "His hair is blond, like your grandfather's." Baby Brother had a lace bonnet tied to his tiny head, and I saw no hair.

I wondered why they hadn't put him to sleep in the crib that rocks but never tips over, in which Claire got to sleep for so long that, one time, I could not help but scratch her face to wake her up. Mémé spanked me for the first time ever, but Maman explained to me that we all got our turn in the crib and that I used to sleep in it too.

That evening, in Maman's room, I wondered why our baby brother was not there. I reached for him, sure I could carry him, since he was almost as small as a doll, but Mémé pulled me away from the desk, saying, "Let him, let him be."

There was no one to say goodbye to in Maman's room. The doctor and his wife had turned their backs to us. They were putting odd-shaped things in a large box, as if the box mattered more than anything. Madame Corentin, usually so kind to us, was unfolding a sheet, her face looking the other way the whole time she was in Maman's room. I asked for Papa, but Mémé said he didn't feel well, that he was smoking in the garden.

I looked at Maman again. She was fast asleep, curled up on her side. She had not moved since we had come in. The lamp near her bed made her face shine even more than usual, as if she was about to

14

smile in her sleep. I wanted to go up to her and touch her face. But all at once, all three of them pushed us toward the door. They gave my shoulders a shove. I did not like it and so I stopped walking. I turned around to go up to her bed, but all I could do was look at Maman one more time. She still had not moved. They pushed me out at last, and closed the door very fast, making me wince.

The next morning the house was full of people, but I could not find Maman. Maybe she was at Mass, like all the other mornings, because I heard Mémé say to the washerwoman, "Yes, she's gone."

Yet the church beadle himself was in our house, hanging silver and black cloth over the doorway. He put candlesticks, much taller than myself, on the floor, next to a wooden seaman's trunk that looked like one of our grandfather's in the attic.

I ran up and down the house trying to find more church things.

15

People came into the dining room holding large bunches of flowers. They didn't smile and hardly talked as they handed them to Mémé. "God bless your daughter's soul, Madame." But Mémé kept forgetting to say thank you. The farmers and their wives, on their way to the market, brought slabs of butter, with flowers, wheels and suns grooved on top. Some also left loaves of black bread. Mémé, who likes butter a lot, didn't even look at the table, with no room left for one more gift.

The barber's wife handed her flowers made of tiny beads the color of rain, saying, "In remembrance. It can't ever fade." And she wiped tears off her nose. Not long ago, her husband cut Maman's beautiful long hair, for all they want is people's hair to make wigs. I saw Maman sit in their shop, with all the cut hair on the floor and I ran to hide in the fields till dark, because Maman told me, "Run back home now," when I started to cry.

16

I didn't feel sad at all to see the barber's wife cry, but she should not have come to our house to do it, annoying Mémé so much with her chatter and her tears that Mémé herself made a funny face and started weeping.

Just as I was having a good time with Augustine, playing hide and seek inside the big folds of the black and silver cloth, the doctor's wife arrived to take us to her house up the street. I didn't like the doctor's house. I got lost in it many times. There is a large trap door in the floor, right in the middle of the hallway. It goes to the wine cellar, one of the doctor's children told me. I was afraid to walk on it, fall and be buried alive, the way the old neighbor Coz throws the newborn cats down the deep well in front of our house. The doctor's children told me that, they get punished sometimes, and they have to stay down in the cellar all afternoon. At home we hardly ever get punished. When he is home, Papa tells us nice stories, over and over again, and he never scolds us.

17

Chapter Three

We had to stay at the doctor's house for days. No one would tell us why we couldn't leave. The five children all acted like babies, except Monique, who is just a little older than me. She is like a mother, and she changes her little brother's diapers all the time. I feel sorry for her, she never has time to play.

In the evening, the doctor's wife, who is fat and soft, let me climb on her lap while she read us the story of an aviator's little blond friend. He couldn't find his way back to a rose he loved more than anything else in the universe. He got lost in the desert, where a snake bit him and he fell asleep, like Maman.

My baby brother flew up to a star called Limbo. I don't know if he was looking for anything. I know that I don't really miss him. With Maman it's different; she's lost and can't find her way back to our house. All the time I was at the doctor's house, I longed to be back home and check Maman's room.

But we had to stay, and night and day started to feel the same, for everything is grey in the doctor's house, except for the white beds and the white kitchen. But even at night everything there became much blacker than anything in our house. At home, the tables and the chairs break their legs easily, but our things are yellow, red, blue, and it was always warm in Maman's room. In the evening, near the fireplace, she sewed our school outfits and our clothes. We had to wear the same old clothes over and over, because of the war Papa told us. But she had not finished sewing our new dolls before she left. Papa had painted the faces. Maman said that she would let me have the doll with-the blue dress, and Augustine would have the red one. The other dolls were for the charity fair.

All three of us refused to eat the doctor's food. It smelled too much of ether in the dining room, right next to his office, and I had to hold my nose. Not long ago Maman carried me in there. I slept in Maman's arms for a long time after. We had to say Grace before each meal, give thanks for the mountains of dripping greens, for the hard lentils with their tiny pebbles that got stuck in my gums. I always hoped that there would be none left when my turn came to hand over my plate, for I had never eaten such awful food. I made little stacks all around my plate, and underneath it, too. I kept a ball of food inside my mouth to go and spit outside when the meal was over.

Later, the doctor told Mémé that we had horrible table manners. But it was not Claire's fault if she cried the whole time she had to be in the dining room. The food scared her. At home, she eats only cream of wheat. And when the doctor scolded Augustine because of the food she put inside her apron pocket, she pretended not to hear him. Except once, she yelled back, "I hate rabbit food." She got up from her chair without waiting to be excused, telling the doctor she hated him as well. He blushed but pretended he had not heard her. So she was not given any jam, the only thing she liked, for dessert.

I am sure that the doctor guessed that if he put her down the wine cellar she would break every bottle in there. For lately Augustine scares everybody, except Mémé who calls her "my sweet Dou-Dou." After I was born she had to become Mémé's baby. I was born right on top of Augustine, Maman told me once. That's why she is extra fat and I'm extra thin.

Since we are back home, and Maman is lost, I get punished by Mémé just like the doctor's children, and I get no dessert. But Mémé would never make us go to the coal closet, even though she says she will. When I don't want to eat and I get up from the table, she tells Susie to catch me one way and Augustine the other way, around and around the

21

table. Yesterday, I got so angry because of it that I pulled the oilcloth down on the floor, with everything on it. It was so scary to feel so angry that I was glad to be sent to bed early.

Today I raced snails on the shiny parquet in Maman's room. We aren't supposed to go inside but I do it anyway. Mémé scolded me again. "Only you could think of that, disgusting snails on your Maman's floor. If she could see you. You're impossible, I tell you, you give me so much work." Mémé doesn't understand about the silence in Maman's room. The yellow curtains are always drawn shut now, making sunshine in the room, even when it rains outside. The snails were moving so slowly, trailing their silver threads. They're beautiful. They can never get lost. I am sure that they know things I don't know yet.

Mémé doesn't want me to understand anything. That's why she keeps scolding me.

After lunch, Augustine and Claire cried an awful lot because Mémé wouldn't let them go into Maman's room. Augustine got so mad she started kicking the door. So I sat on the floor next to her, to tell her what I'd guessed, watching the snails. Maman isn't really lost. For if Maman went to the woods that evening and got lost, she is still there. I don't understand why Maman went into the woods, all by herself, because she always took us with her. I told Augustine that I would go and find Maman in the woods. But she only screamed and cried more. Claire started to cry again, just to be like Augustine.

I don't cry much, except when I fall, running down the rocky path coming out of our garden. The blood scares me then, and my tears help me not to look at my knees full of tiny gravel right under the skin.

One thing I don't understand is why Papa tells people on the street, "I have lost my wife," as if he believed he'll never see Maman again. He has no time to look for her. He has to leave very early in the morning to make the rounds of the farms on his creaky bicycle, sometimes going as far as forty kilometers in the rainstorms.

I'm not sure why Mémé likes to take us to the cemetery every day, except on the days when it rains. She has us dressed neatly, with the help of Thérèse, saying, "Your Maman wants to see you look nice." But Maman got lost in the woods, and if she could see us, she would come back.

We play on the stone edges of the tombs while Mémé changes the flowers on ours. Mémé calls it "my daughter's grave" when she meets people on the street on our way to the cemetery, but our mother never took us to see it and our father never comes either. I don't like our tomb. It is the newest one. It has no stone edge to stand on, no wreath with tiny silver and violet beads with "Eternal Kisses" spelled on it; it has no marble book opened at "Always Beloved" or "Till We Meet in Heaven," written in letters of gold. Augustine reads them aloud as we skip along. No one is supposed to touch things on the tombs, otherwise I would put everything I like best on our tomb, for there is nothing on it, except ugly metal vases that keep falling when the ocean storms start blowing.

Mémé said the other day that she can't bear to look at those small marble angels on some of the other tombs. They don't have to be played with, like dolls always needing to be dressed and undressed. They are like babies at the beach in the summer. The rain bathes them, and they become very shiny, like pebbles at the edge of the sea.

It is the crosses with Jesus nailed to them that I hate. We're lucky our tomb doesn't have one. We have a wooden cross instead, with "March 6, 1944" painted in black, but no Jesus. I try not to look at the rows of concrete crosses with Jesus, but I can't help noticing that Our Savior looks a bit different on each one, except for that crown of thorns.

Why do people make tombs?" Is Jesus everyone's beloved? Because he is naked, like a baby, with only a tattered diaper to cover him? Then, why is he nailed down like those insects the doctor has on his wall? Why do they hurt him?

This evening in the kitchen, our father told Mémé, in a rough voice, "Your dear friend, that doctor of yours, he's an ass, just good enough to deliver cows at the farms." I'm glad Papa does not like the doctor either. To save having to buy the newspaper, he gets it from Mémé every afternoon, after she has read everything in it. Then the doctor and her drink fresh coffee and talk a lot about the war and the Liberation. But this evening, Papa was very angry at the doctor. "If I see that worm, I'll kick him in the ass. Even a cow he wouldn't have let bleed for five hours, and goddam it, what about Monsieur Viol's car? Even the Germans would have lent one to go to Lorient." Mémé's whole face shook when she answered, "and what about you, Holy Samaritan all right, where were you?" I am sure they

26

were talking about Maman's blood. She was badly hurt, the evening before she got lost.

Chapter Four

I don't like staying in the house now. When it rains, I go to Maman's room. I turn the door handle as softly as I can and I walk on tiptoes, trying not to make the floor creak, especially if Mémé is in the kitchen down below. I open the window and lean far beyond the blue windowsill, stretching my hand out. I call for a ladybug to land on it and to please tell me no lies about the weather or anything I want to know. But the ladybug always flies off before I can finish counting to twenty. Maybe it guesses that I can't quite count to twenty.

Since Maman got lost I've been going to school. Sister Josepha teaches me to count with little sticks of wood. When so many are lined up on the desk, it makes a number. But it is very hard to choose the right one. I know so little yet.

It rains almost every day now. I play with the things in Maman's sewing basket. I try to sew a button, but it ends up upside down, dangling from a bunch of tangled thread. And I've tried to finish the sleeve on our baby brother's little jacket. I messed it all up instead. Papa told me that he would teach me to knit. He learned how to do it when he was a small boy to make scarves for the soldiers who had gone to war.

Papa does not come home every day since he has rebuilt the bicycle and greased up the gears. The barber gave him two good tires for some eggs. Now that he can ride his bicycle a very long time, he sleeps at the farms and the castles. He comes home if a relative visits, like Cousin Yvette. We had never met Cousin Yvette before. She looks mean with her bright green eyes, which match her green hat. She does not smile at us and tries to look only at Papa.

Just before dinner, when Cousin Yvette was in her room, which is our playroom, Mémé asked Papa, "How many cousins can you have, Mény? This is the third one in two months. And divorced from two sculptors too."

I asked Papa what "divorced from two sculptors" meant. He said that a sculptor is a man who makes statues and that, just like statues can break in two sometimes, married people can do the same thing. "And do they fix the statue, when it's broken?" I asked. But he just laughed a little, saying, "No. Once it's broken, no one can fix it."

At dinner, Cousin Yvette sat at the table where Maman used to sit, so that I thought for a small instant that Maman had gone away never to come

29

back. And then Cousin Yvette scolded Papa, "What is the point of waiting, really? You'll have to think about it, and fast, too." Mémé is the one who answered, "I won't have that kind of talk in this house. Go ahead and marry a third sculptor, but this one here you leave alone." Our cousin turned red but her ears remained white. Her eyes opened as big as the bottom of our well. She threw her fork across the table and it went sliding under the stove. That's probably why her marriages keep breaking, I thought, as she ran upstairs.

Our playroom is now full of green hats, red shoes and purple scarves. Our cousin's bed is right in the middle of the room, with a large mirror leaning against it. Yesterday, when everyone was downstairs, I sat in front of it, and I looked and looked at my face and my body. Even though I don't look like a small child at all, I can't tell if I have grown taller since Maman got lost, or if she would recognize me now, or if she tried to find her way home. I sat very still the whole time, but my face kept changing, just as if lots of new faces wanted to come out at the same time.

I heard the stairs creak and before I could hide Cousin Yvette came in. I ran out, because the last thing I want is to be in the same room with a grown-up who throws forks.

I don't really miss our playroom, because Augustine has smashed all my Christmas dishes, trampling them and saying they were hers. She's turned her stuffed animals inside out and has hidden my doll someplace. She won't tell me where. She screams, "She's lost, lost, you dumbbell...," repeating it over and over again. I told her that I would rather lose all my toys than my brains, like her. She pushed me down the stairs, but I caught hold of the banister before I could fall all the way down. I told her that my brains can't break whatever she does to me, but that all the toys and the doll she's stolen from me can't help her find her smarts.

31

Now she refuses to hold my hand on the way to school, and sometimes I get scared because the cars drive so fast and honk their horns. Papa says people are celebrating the Liberation, which is coming soon, and they're doing stupid things, like driving too fast.

I have learned to count up to fifteen with Sister Josepha and I can write the entire alphabet, except for the last five letters. After our lesson, if she is pleased with us, Sister Josepha lets us polish our black desk with bits of candle wax from the church. I have seen some of the poor children in our class eat their pieces of candle. They live by the beach with their mother, but Mémé says they will never have a father. Their house is a dark barn without windows and their clothes are in tatters. They don't wear any underwear under their torn black dresses. Their heads are full of lice, which the Sisters try to remove. I would not like being poor and cold like them, but they never complain about it. They don't talk to the other children and they refuse to answer Sister Josepha's questions. No one wants to sit next to them because of their lice, and the bad smell. I sometimes end up next to one of them, Denise, because I don't want to look ashamed, or scared. I lend her my pencil and my ruler, and once she gave me two boiled chestnuts she had in her pocket.

Augustine is a year older than me, so she's in the next class with Sister Amélie, but she can't write too well yet. This morning, when Sister Amélie hung Augustine's purple ink-stained notebook on her back and made her walk around the schoolyard during recess, I went over to her and I chased the laughing children away. Augustine was crying so hard that her eyes could not even open anymore. I took her hand in mine and I walked with her. The children stopped jeering. When the bell rang at the end of the recess, I asked her to run away to the woods with me, but she wouldn't. Instead she walked back inside, holding her writing notebook tight. I know that I would have run away if Sister Josepha did that to me. But she's much nicer than Sister Amélie. Sister Josepha is almost a young girl

33

and she smiles a lot and sings to us. It is easy to learn with her because she never scolds me, even when I don't get it right the first time.

Every evening before we fall asleep, Mémé makes us pray. "Little darling Maman who is in Heaven, bless and protect your beloved children." In the cemetery she also speaks to our mother as she arranges the dahlias in vases, "My beloved one, my little one, may we be reunited in God." She often misses the vase when she pours the water, "Sapristi! My beloved saint." She invents everything as she goes along; her prayers are not like the ones we have to say at school. I can never remember how they go and it makes me feel very tired to pray, first thing in the morning, instead of playing. But Mémé often cries when she prays. I can see that her black veil is wet even though it's not raining.

When will Maman be back? She can't see us from where she is, but does she hear Mémé?

No one sleeps in Maman's room anymore. I detest having to sleep in Mémé's room. My bed is at the foot of her large wooden bed. She can't see me in bed and I can't see her either. But, the other evening I saw her blow out the candle, and I didn't recognize her for a moment because of the long shadows behind her head. It was just because her white hair was all undone, but it made me cringe. Now I make sure I don't look at her when she's about to blow out the candle. Augustine sleeps near the fireplace. Mémé can see her, repeating six times at least each night "tuck yourself in. Don't forget your shoulders." The things Mémé is the most afraid of in the world are the drafts which, she says, sneak up treacherously from everywhere in this barn of a house. Our house is not a barn, even though the entire downstairs was filled with potatoes when our father found it. We had to leave Brest in a hurry because of the airplanes dropping bombs, and we were lucky Papa found this house. It has a stone heart engraved above the door with the date "1757"

35

written on it, and underneath there are mysterious letters. Even the priest doesn't know what they mean.

Claire's crib, with a drawing of Pierrot and the moon on it, is just besides Mémé's bed. All she does is stare wide-eyed at Mémé, sucking her thumb, as if Mémé were the Holy Ghost. Even though she is almost three years old, she has not said one word yet. Maman always said Claire was born "under the bombs," although I'm not sure what she meant.

Because I grind my teeth when I sleep, Augustine calls me an "abominable teeth-grinder," and every evening she makes sure to turn the grimacing ram's head that sits on the mantelpiece so that it faces me. Then, she says, "If you grit your teeth tonight, he'll eat you up, and then you'll be buried alive, just like Father Coz's cats." I never answer her, and I look hard at the light fixture above, all speckled with dust and full of dead flies. Nothing Augustine says makes sense.

I can't help chewing on the tips of my pajama collar when I'm in bed. But Susie told me that she is going to cut all my collars off so that she won't have to mend them. She is sometimes mean, like the time she slammed the kitchen door on my fingers. Because she is the eldest, she has the middle room all to herself. There are bullet holes all over the dresser, from the time we had to run into the woods to hide because the Germans said that they were going to burn down the village. That time, only Augustine was not afraid of the Germans. She became furious and hollered that she wouldn't leave until she finished all her mashed potatoes. Augustine loves to eat more than anything. Mémé had to drag her on her knees, all the way to the woods. I ran along with Maman as she pushed Claire's carriage full of food and silver forks and spoons. We stayed for several days in a stone cottage in the woods which the people who live in the castle lent to our father. We all slept on the floor, except Claire. The lady from the castle brought her a

37

wooden crib carved with the most beautiful flowers, stars, rabbits, and fawns. I wanted to sleep in it so badly, I almost made Claire fall out of it trying to climb in. It was big enough for three babies, but Maman wouldn't let me. We ate cherries the whole time we were in the woods because there was no kitchen in the tiny house, only garden tools. We heard a lot of gunshots and we saw thick smoke rising above the trees, near the village.

On the way back to our house we saw the black carcass of an airplane, and Papa said that both pilots had burned in it. The Germans only burned three houses that time, but they shot bullets through every window of our house. When we came back, old Father Coz told Mémé that he had removed the pile of wood the Germans had stacked at the entrance of our house and put out the fire, just in time. Mémé was so glad he had saved our house that she gave him ten francs to buy himself his favorite bottle of wine.

Augustine's mashed potatoes were still on the kitchen table, and she screamed when she saw them, all grey and mildewed. Since that day, whenever she sees a German soldier on the street, she calls him "You rotten mildewy rat." She's lucky they don't understand French. "La Marseillaise" is the only French they understand and they have forbidden anyone from singing it. But when Susie and her best friend go up to the attic, they sing it as loud as they can. When Mémé isn't home, they even open up the dormer window all the way up so everyone can hear. Maybe that's why the soldiers shot our house full of bullets.

Susie never lets us enter her room. She sits for hours on her bed, talking to her girlfriend, the grocer's daughter. And I saw Susie exchange our Christmas tree decorations for ribbons and hairpins. Mémé keeps telling her that she must help more around the house, because Maman has said so. Susie yells back, "No one is going to take my freedom away. And Maman is where she can't even talk. I carried at least a hundred pails of water up to Maman's room that day, that's enough work for a lifetime." But it isn't freedom that Susie wants the most, its new dresses, the tighter the better, and curlers for her hair. She is so worried about her hair or that she'll tear her skirts that she won't even jump rope anymore.

In the morning, Claire's sheets have to be aired on the windowsill, but the room smells bad anyway. I get up as fast as I can and go down to the kitchen to play with the cats, behind the stove. It is cold before Thérèse arrives to light the fire. The small cats refuse to be taken out of their box where they are warm next to their sleeping mother. Thérèse arrives with the two pails of water from the well. First, she saws enough wood for the day and builds the fire. Then she boils the milk and washes the dishes. On Sundays, Thérèse sings in the church. They say she has the voice of an angel. And some mornings she sings for me in the kitchen. She sings in Breton but it doesn't matter that I don't understand the words because her voice is so beautiful. It's like the gentle sea breeze, pushing the big black clouds so the sun can shine. Sometimes she makes the sun come out, just like at the beach when it's too cold to undress but then the sun breaks through.

The other morning, I could not help talking to Thérèse about Maman being lost in the woods. And I asked her if the woods were very big and if she knew all the hidden paths, since she was born in a little house just at the edge of the woods. But she would not tell me. "Listen Vivi, you imagine too much. Next Sunday, I'll come to get you after church and you and I shall play the organ together at my house." I know that to imagine is to see real images inside one's head. Like when Papa tells us stories. I can always see what he talks about. I see the Beast's castle, deep in the forest, and I see Blandine walking day and night, trying to find the eglantine bush. It's as if I had seen it all, someplace, long ago. It's the same in my head when I think about Maman. I can see her walking, and then losing her way in the

41

woods. And I want to go find her, and more than, anything else, take her hand and lead her back to our house.

I asked Thérèse, "Will you take me deep into the woods, to look for Maman?" But this time, she frowned, "Go and play, Vivi. I have work to do." I couldn't play. Instead I went outside and sat on a stone. I watched Madame Herbet, the cobbler's wife, stir her boiling laundry water and feed the fire underneath her huge pot. Her yard touches ours, and I made sure I stayed on our side, because she pretends not to know our names. She has ten children already, so she cannot stand any of us, especially Augustine for some reason. She yells at her sometimes, the way she yells at her own children. She works so hard that she's become very tall and very thin. Mémé says that Madame Herbet is "no better than a rabbit, the way she has children one after the other. What with her red-hot drunk of a husband, no wonder—just good enough to make clogs, red-headed babies, and those coffins." I asked

Mémé what a coffin was. She gave me a strange look. "A box...for the priest." I wanted to know more, but Mémé said that I ask too many questions.

Chapter Five

Every morning, Mémé goes into Maman's room to put her hair up, sitting in front of the big mirror for a long time. Everything is still the same, except the way the bed is made, just to stop anyone from lifting up the covers and climbing in. Maman's paintings of flowers and of the sea are on the walls, except for the one with the lilacs which our father took down, and brought to his room on the third floor. Mémé was very annoyed with him, for she does not want anything changed. I know that Maman's hair is inside a long golden box, but it's locked so I cannot lift the cover. I wish they had never cut Maman's hair. Her ivory hairbrush and comb are still lying inside the dark metal dish, in front of the mirror. All around the edge of it there is a woman's body, swept by the waves. Her face is smiling as if she were not scared. I would be terribly scared if a wave came at me, before I had even learned to swim, which is a long, long way off, since the ocean is so cold that I can only stay in it one minute at a time. I wonder why grownups like scary things, like this dish. Even our mother never swam, and Mémé never entered the ocean either, she told us. I wish Papa had also taken this dish to his room.

All Maman's things are waiting for her, even the moonstone necklace I once broke, pulling too hard on it when I was in her arms. Mémé had the barber's wife repair it. Now, Maman's things are all covered with dust and Mémé's long white hair, since she keeps her powder box and smell-good puff on Maman's desk. She talks to Maman while she combs her hair, then lifts it up the way the woman has it on the dish. She tells Maman that she'll bring her the red and purple dahlias the grocer's wife gives us all the time, "two bunches, Madeleine darling. I'd rather it does not rain today. You'll like them, the others need changing." Mémé thinks that our mother is in Heaven with God. She also thinks that the only way to get there is by going through the cemetery. But at other times, when she can't tie the black velvet ribbon that holds the wrinkled skin tight around her neck, she says, "Will you give me a hand, Vivi?" I tie it up for her, but she never says thanks. Instead, she goes on talking to Maman about what she'll buy at the butcher's for our lunch, as if she were in the room listening.

I have learned to climb the ladder up to the attic. Lately, Augustine and I have been playing among the piles of old things. The books, the photographs, our grandfather's papers and letters have spilled all over the floor. Within the mess, we build beautiful rooms for our mother's large porcelain dolls. Her parents bought them when she was as small as we are now. They have faces as real as babies. We put them to sleep in the bed- rooms inside the house we've built. No noise for a long, long while, just silence. Then the rain begins to whisper again on the roof, above our heads. One of the cats springs up from a corner, knocking down an old vase, barely missing the bucket that is almost full of water, under the roof-leak.

Once, our father told the doctor that he regretted he had brought everything all the way from Brest in a truck, and during the bombing too. "Every scrap of useless paper, every rusty basin, fifty hatboxes, piles of *Illustration* my damn mother-in-law wanted—all of it! Our house was the only one left standing on the Cours d'Ajots and she made me go back under the bombs, five times! All those school notebooks, and the kitchen sink."

Sometimes, when our dolls are sleeping, I look at the old books, many of them torn and full of worm eggs. But it is *Illustration*, full of pictures, that I love most. Except the one with the pictures of Hitler in it. Even though he looks like a regular man and not a devil, I tore his picture in many tiny pieces and let them drown in the yellow rain water in the bucket. He bombed Brest when I was still a baby. Mémé told me that I had to spend the whole day in a bomb shelter being sick because the milk the Red Cross gave us was not good for me.

Uncle Raymond's notebooks are full of short lines, sometimes in different colors of ink. The notebooks are called "Poems by Raymond R." He also made a lot of drawings of a bear called Count Michu, being made prisoner by savages dressed in feathers and fur, or sailing on huge ships. In one drawing, the bear has been killed and is tied to a

47

pole. I heard Mémé worry out loud about Uncle Raymond. "A poet should not have had five children, agronomist or not." We have never seen our cousins because they live in Free France. We are refugees here in the village. The Germans occupy it and they have buried landmines on the beaches. One little boy was lost one day, I heard Papa tell Mémé. His father was Gautrin, the crab fisherman. His father went and shot a German soldier. "Where is the little boy now?" I asked Papa, and "What did the Germans do to his father?" But Papa would not tell me because Mémé began to scold him: "Meny, stop it. You know that children don't belong in this cruel war. You've no right."

"Hitler does not look at it quite that way," Papa answered.

But Mémé got angry: "Don't you dare, in front of the children!"

Chapter Six

A flea stings my calf and I scream. The dolls wake up and we go downstairs again. We always go outside after the rain. It smells of the sea and of moss and tree bark. The sun turns the air the color of fresh lilacs; it gives a bright silver rim to the wet slates on the roof—and the edges of the flying clouds. But it does not last long, and everything turns grey again. Sometimes, just before nightfall, a very fine orange and pink powder quietly falls to the ground, and in the dusk it smells of camphor and blooming lilies. As it gets dark, the scent fills up our garden. It is like the inside of a church under the trees. I go to sit under the hazel tree, on a bench Papa made for Maman. I would like to fall asleep on it and never have to go back to my bed in Mémé's smelly room! I chew on a single hazel nut for .a long time, not cracking it open. I tell myself stories about what moves inside it. It could be a house full of comfy rooms where children play all day long. It could be a magic forest full of hidden trails with soft green moss on the ground and primroses all over. It could be anything, even the huge night sky with the stars falling. Or it could just be a mean, ugly dwarf with long dirty nails.

I have never told Augustine about the bench under the hazel tree. It is the only secret spot I have. I pretend I have gone to the outhouse when they ask me where I have been in the near dark. And my soup is almost cold on my plate.

We go down to the cemetery every afternoon if it doesn't rain. We all go, except Susie who says that she has too much homework.

I carry the water pitcher and fill it at the village pump on the way. Often, when we reach the black steel gate, I stop because of the high hedges of blue hydrangeas blending with the blue of the sky. I want to look at them forever. Mémé says that we are not allowed to take any flowers. If I could, I would cover our tomb with bunches of blue hydrangeas to make a sky door. But I have to listen to Mémé. She is so old, and I don't want to upset her.

Already, she could not look worse with her black veil falling over her black hat, covering her whole face. Her hands shake when she has to lean down to change the flowers. I carried the water pitcher, but when I skipped along on the edges of the tombs, half the water spilled out and now Mémé scolds me. Sometimes I can't eat for days.

After she's finished her prayers and we've all made the sign of the cross, I rush to the dump to throw away the faded flowers. It smells of rot and Augustine refuses to go near it. My sisters don't help Mémé, I don't know why. She does a lot of things to please them, but they just scream and cry a lot, and

51

she lets them carry on. With me, it is just the opposite. The more I try to help her, the more she yells at me, the way she does with Papa. Maybe it's because I remind her of Papa. He told her he was going to leave after the Liberation. Mémé got angry. "And don't come back too soon either." I don't know why she's always mean to him.

One afternoon, after we returned home from the cemetery, we found our beds back in Maman's room, and her bed was missing. Mémé says that it's in the attic. Did Maman tell her to do it, all the way from where she is? Why doesn't Mémé ever talk about Maman finding the way back to our house?

In the evening I get very sick because I have eaten old baptism candies I found in Maman's desk drawer. They were in a round box, pale blue with a silver angel on top. I lifted the cover; it was almost weightless, the way a cloud must be. At first, the candies didn't taste like anything. But I can't explain anything at all to Mémé, she scolds me too fast. "Oh, you're the toughest one of all, always giving me extra chores. Really, Vivi, Couldn't you see they were rotten?" I can't answer Mémé because I just want to throw up. She sends for the doctor and she puts me in bed with a very heavy china basin right on my aching stomach. Thérèse and she wrap towels around me. All the while, Mémé continues to scold me. "They were at least four months old. Your Maman and I bought them for the baby's baptism." I don't answer Mémé because she does not understand anything, doesn't see that I have become different. I just want to close my eyes tight, to block the tears. My stomach hurts as if someone was hitting me from inside. But Mémé can hardly see me through her eyeglasses, all stained with soup and dust. And I am too sick to tell her that the candies looked as smooth as the moon. Some were pale blue, others pink, and I swallowed all those. At least I didn't eat the white ones, because they smelled like old mushrooms. I thought, maybe they're meant only for the babies who don't get baptized and go

53

directly to Limbo, and one should not eat those. The first one tasted like a whiff of crushed ants when I bit into it. But I didn't spit it out. Instead, I closed my eyes and I rolled my tongue around each one, so I could swallow them whole. I closed my eyes, and imagined it was Maman who was putting the candy in my mouth, like the priest at Communion. Except that we had just come back from Baby Brother's baptism, and Maman was telling me a secret: she would always take me with her, wherever she went.

Then, much later, Augustine walked into the room and she ran out fast to tell Mémé about the candies all over the desk, and me crouching on the floor, not talking and breathing badly because of the pain.

The doctor comes to make me throw up the candy. He tells me to swallow a raw egg with some awful medicine in it. After, I really fell ill, and I have a big white lump where they say my stomach is.

Why were the candies so smooth-looking, like pearls?

Chapter Seven

My baby brother has flown to Limbo, where everything is white, where the moon shines always instead of the sun, so that the baby angels can sleep peacefully. Just outside the gate, the pink and blue clouds feel like cushions when one sits on them, waiting for the door to open up a bit. I want to enter it so badly, but someone kicks the door closed again.

I wake up and Susie is by my bed, whispering, "You bad, bad girl. Look at your pajama collar." I chewed off a big chunk of it as I slept, to get rid of the awful taste in my mouth.

They come in to change my pajamas. I'm cold with sweat. I cry. I cry because I'm scared, trying to decide if I want to get well again, or never wake up. They also change my pillow, soaked with tears and sweat. I fall asleep again, and I wake up scared, not knowing my mind anymore, what it is I want. In my dreams the white angels change into green devils. I cry for Maman to come and help me brush my teeth to get rid of the awful taste, but she doesn't hear me. I don't know where she went.

Now they put her red bathrobe over my blanket. I am cold and I am burning hot all night. Maman's bathrobe glows red with blood several times. I scream for help. No one hears me. I fall asleep for good when I see the daylight in between the folds of the yellow curtains. I am in Maman's room, like before she got lost. I do not want to wake up, ever again, that's why I let myself fall asleep at last.

Is it the next day that Papa at last returns from the farms? He places a basket of raspberries next to me on the covers. It hurts my whole head to keep my eyes open, but I can see that the raspberries are the same color as Maman's bathrobe. I eat them but I cannot taste them at all. On my tongue, they feel like a hundred tiny sponges full of clean rain, and they soothe me inside.

Mémé enters the room and scolds Papa for feeding me the raspberries. "You really want to make her ill again?" Papa says nothing. "The doctor said bouillon, only bouillon." She doesn't see the soft sunshine in the room because of her dirty eyeglasses. The warm light makes the raspberries glow like tiny drops of blood when you prick your finger with a needle. Mémé arranges my pillow and the whole basket empties on Maman's bathrobe. Papa picks them up one by one and feeds them to me. Mémé does not want to see that I am cured, and she cannot see Papa's face. One of his cheeks is wet with tears. He lets go of my hand and leaves the room, without a word. I close my eyes, and behind them I see something I have never seen before. It is the inside of a giant snail. I am inside it and I climb each groove, like a staircase. It goes around and around — gold, orange, red. I can rest as long as I want inside the grooves. And no one can find me there. I glide up and down, and it is the best thing I have ever felt. Even better than bathing in the sea on a hot day.

I fall asleep for a long time, rocking gently inside the snail's giant belly, and there is no end, no beginning. When I wake up, it is evening and the yellow curtains are dark, like wood. More than anything, I wish that no one should enter the room, ever again. But just then Augustine opens the door and comes in. The first thing she sees is the nearly empty basket of raspberries, for I have kept a few, for their beautiful color. She teases me, calling me a "red tiger" because I won't let her have any. And she says, "You should see your red whiskers, too. Really, what an ugly tiger you make." Do I really look like a tiger? I get up to look at myself in Maman's mirror. The mirror lies, or is it true that I have changed so much? I'm not red at all, I am very white, except for my red mouth. When I go back to bed, I see that Augustine has taken the basket of raspberries and is running out of the room. My eyes can only see a large white cloud. I shut my eyes. Under Maman's bathrobe it is no longer red, but very black. It smells of dust and blood. I wish someone would come now and give me some light. I know that I am not a tiger, it is just that I have become different.

Now I have to put my hands over my ears, not to have to listen to Augustine who has come back, asking me to play with her. I take a large breath and roll on my side. I smell Maman's blood, or maybe it is my fingers' old blood on her bathrobe. I want to fall asleep, and never wake up. I know that I have started to live again, and shall continue, tomorrow. I'll look the same to everyone, but inside I am someone else.

The next day, Mémé and Thérèse wash me from head to foot, in the large basin set on the floor of Maman's room. Mémé says that I have to wear a corset because the doctor said that I have the beginning of a hernia, that is, a bump in the middle of my stomach. Under the corset they have wrapped me up in a tight bandage, just like Mémé does every morning for the veins on her legs. And even though it is warm outside, I have to wear a woolen undershirt, a petticoat, a skirt, long socks and a sweater. I can hardly move with all the layers. And I have to go to school looking as fat as a cider barrel.

Already, Mémé is scolding me. "No running in the fields after school, you hear me?"

Chapter Eight

The best game after school is to try to throw one's enemies in the nettles. The boys from the public school join in the game and they chase us with sticks, screaming, "Go visit Hell, you little saints... go say hello to the devil for us." I never let myself get hit by their sticks. I have a lot of fun after school. Sometimes a few of us go to the cherry orchard. We climb the trees and eat all we can, till it gets dark.

A few days later, my clothes are torn and most of my buttons are missing. Mémé says that she is giving up on me. I have hidden the corset and the bandage in the coal closet, but I told her that I have lost them. "How could you lose your undergarments? Only you could do that!" I don't care. I would rather be scolded every day than have to wear a corset and a bandage around my stomach.

It is the first time that I lie, like grown-ups when they don't want children to guess something. I often guess when they are lying, but somehow Mémé did not guess that I was lying. I don't like it, and my throat half closes around my lie, as if it wanted to stop my fib from leaving my mouth. But Mémé just mumbles, "I give up, I give up on you."

I have to go to the fields to play after school. My legs have to run. "Why can't you be like the others, come back to your doll?" Mémé says. I try to explain that it's nice in the fields. Besides, someone has to go get the milk at the mill, since Augustine never wants to go and Susie has too much homework. So Mémé finally stops scolding me.

Sometimes, I glimpse Lilimoumoute, almost hidden behind the trees, walking with his tiny dog. He lives in the woods under a giant oak tree. Susie says that he is half man and half woman, and that no one wants him to enter the village. That's why his parents sent him to live in the woods when he was very small. Susie giggles when she tells me about Lilimoumoute. She is a silly girl. Lilimoumoute looks sad and lost even though he knows the woods better than anyone. He wears a sheepskin and a priest's black hat, and his very long hair covers his face. But I can tell that his cheeks are just as smooth as a baby's, and that he'll never grow old. He can't talk—he only grunts. And he barks just like his dog when the boys throw stones at him. The children run away as fast as they can. They are all afraid of him, but I am not.

Chapter Nine

Papa does not come home very often now. And he stays in the kitchen as little as possible since Mémé scolds him all the time. Even the day he brought back five dozen eggs and was totally drenched because of the rainstorm, she scolded, "Oh, don't complain. You've a jolly life all right." Papa brings back butter, which she likes a lot, and he always finds a piece of ham for us, or else the farmer gives us five kilos of potatoes on market day. I helped Papa stack the five dozen eggs in a beautiful pile on the table. We wrapped up three dozen, one by one, and packed them in tin boxes for his mother and brothers who are in Paris, starving because of the war.

Sometimes Papa takes all three of us to his room on the third floor. First he burns bits of scented paper to get rid of the awful tobacco smell. But he always rolls himself a new cigarette, with old butts, right after. Then we sit, all three of us, on his knees inside his large armchair. He tells us stories about the monkey Caramel and Patapouf the cat. His mother, who is blind and whom we have never seen, has sent a fairy tale about a girl called Blandine who got lost in the woods while looking for an eglantine bush, which led her to an enchanted castle where a frightening man-beast lived by himself. Blandine was not scared of the beast because she felt sorry for him. Augustine hated the story, and ran out. She is scared of animals, like the wolf with shiny eyes in the big book of fables Mémé lets us look at sometimes. Augustine begs me to warn her when the page with the wolf is coming up so she can shut her eyes. Sometimes I don't tell her in time, and she screams and hits me. When its bedtime, she always turn the Chinese ram vase towards me, but I don't care.

On Sundays, Papa takes me along to help him with his puppet show. He has stitched their costumes himself, and he painted their faces different colors. He carries everything in a big heavy suitcase. We set up the stage in a barn or in the back room of a church. Papa hides low behind the opening. When he whispers to me, "Now!" I pull open the stage curtain he made with one of Maman's blue dresses. Or I hand him the lighted matches which he quickly sticks in the holes of the Green Devil's ears. The children scream and jump up and down, and the adults put both their hands over their mouth to keep from laughing. My father's voice seems to come from deep below the earth, where Hell is supposed to be. Now I know that it's not true about Hell, way down in the earth, and it's not true about Paradise way up in the sky, either.

After the show is over, I carry a tin box around and the audience drops coins in it. Often they drop old coins from before the war, because they make the same noise as the new ones. Papa decided to start collecting coins, a hundred years old and much older, like those of the kings of France and Rome that the farmers find in the fields. Papa loves to tell me about the history of France, and a place called Versailles. He says our ancestors were nobles, whatever that means. That's why he called me Marie-Antoinette, like the last Queen of France. But no one calls me that, since she lost her head.

One time, Papa took me to see the priest to get more coins because during mass the churchgoers also drop the old coins no one wants. But Papa said, "Thank you, I'm taking these coins because you're kind enough to give them to me. Just one thing: your religion you can keep." And Papa smiled his mean half-smile. At that moment, I didn't want to be his daughter and I wanted to run out of the church as fast as I could, but Papa knew it so he held my hand in his big hard fingers that have become so strong from riding his bicycle all day long.

I know why he won't go to church, even though Mémé scolds him a lot about it. He tells her, "The Pope is an ignoramus. Dominus vobiscums and miserere nobis's are for church mice."

"And you, you belong in Hell," she answers, trembling lightly like a willow leaf about to be carried away by the breeze. "You knew, you knew that the doctor had always said 'one, one child only,' and you, you. . ." Mémé's voice rattles and she loses her words at times like that, and she has to sit down. Maybe that's why, when Mémé gets annoyed at me, she sometimes calls me "the extra one." She thinks that I should not have been born, yet she sometimes talks about our baby brother as if she missed him a lot. "His hair would have been blond, like Pépé's, and a first son, too." If I got lost she wouldn't miss me and she wouldn't talk to the people on the street, saying, "Her hair was black, just like her father's, and a third daughter, too." People don't really like all children, only some of them, those that are not extras. Except Papa, he loves us all. But when he calls out after lunch, "Who wants to come to the farms with me today?" I am the only one who answers "Me, I want to!" and I rush into the house to get the pillow for the back seat of Papa's bicycle. Meanwhile, my sisters go on playing in front of the house as if they hadn't heard him.

Sometimes it rains hard on the roads and Papa makes me sit on the crossbar, in front of him. He puts his large hands over mine on the handlebar. I hardly get wet that way and I help him ride the bike. At the farms, I have to be careful not to slip into the puddles of manure right in front of the doorstep. Often, Papa has to carry me in. The farmers all wear heavy wooden shoes stuffed with straw inside. They are careful to remove them before they enter their kitchen, where they put on black slippers. I can see that they never wash their feet, they are so yellow and black. The smell of the manure doesn't bother them either. It's very dark inside, and the floor is made of hard dirt. But there is always a large fire in the chimney and the food is cooking in very heavy black pots. At mealtime, the farmers ask us to stay. We all eat the gruel out of a wooden bowl. A whole slab of butter floats in the middle of it. Everyone dips a spoon in the gruel, back and forth, and I stand on the bench to reach the bowl. It is the very best food I have ever tasted. Farmers eat in silence. They don't have to eat horsemeat like us at home, or the fish no one buys at the market. I refuse to eat meat; it is what I hate most in the world.

Farmers don't like to talk, except sometimes about the number of cows, pigs, and horses they have. They don't mind the war, but they mind when Papa asks them how much food they can spare for the rest of France. After we have left the farms, Papa often says, "I wonder how many pigs they let out when they saw us coming? Black marketeers all right, the whole bleeding lot of them!"

The other day, Papa drank a whole bottle of fresh cider with a farmer. He started to talk too loud, saying "To hell with doctors, to hell with priests and the Pope." This he repeated at least three times. Another time, when the farmer's wife had said, "This little girl should have stayed home with her Mama," because my clothes were drenched and she had to dry them by the fire after having wrapped me in her shawl, Papa answered, "Grandma has enough to do as it is with the others. I lost my wife last March." I quickly climbed up the bench to reach Papa's ear, and I whispered my secret to him, "Papa, don't tell them about Maman being lost, because I'll go look for her, soon, in the woods. " But Papa laughed at me, just like his Green Devil puppet.

That evening, I slept in the farm kitchen, inside one of the bed cupboards. I would not let Papa close the sliding door, and in the morning there were chickens on my bed, clucking and pecking around my head. The farmer's wife shooed them away but they had laid three eggs right on the quilt. Papa

71

asked the farm woman if he could boil me one for breakfast, "like an English breakfast." The farmer grunted, "Goddam the English and the Americans, and those bombs they're dropping. One of my cows got blown up the other day. I found a single horn, nothing else." He meant the bombs to liberate France from the Germans. Papa told me later that many farmers don't mind being occupied by the Germans because their butter is worth gold.

Another night we stayed to sleep at a castle after a terrible storm on the road. As I fell asleep crying, Papa put his head next to mine on the pillow. The lady of the castle had not let me hold her baby. She had said, "But your daughter has lice," as I was kneeling on the floor next to her baby boy.

A day later, Mémé sent for the barber's wife and she treated our hair with a smelly lotion. Mémé says that we have lice because of the war. At school I sit next to Denise, but the farmers' daughters also have lice. Mémé is upset, and it is the very first time I hear her say that she is glad our Maman can't see us now.

The lotion stings my scalp and the steel comb hurts it even more. Augustine chases her live lice on her school slate. She kills them with a pencil, pretending it is a sword and the lice are giant monsters. Then she spins them and drowns them in the water pail.

Chapter Ten

The Liberation is here at last. It is silver tinsel, which the Americans sprinkle from their airplanes, and all the children run up and down the village street to find bits of it. And there are gunshots coming from the woods. The houses have French flags planted in front one day but not the next, because the Germans reappear to make believe that they have not lost the war. A few days after the Germans have left for good, the Americans arrive in their jeeps in the church square. My father holds me up in his arms. An American soldier sees me all the way from the top of his jeep and he says, "Kiss me quick, kiss me quick." Papa holds me up higher and higher, saying, "Hurry, Vivi, he wants to kiss you." Papa understands English because before he met Maman he spent an entire year in Mississippi, teaching English. The soldier smells of burnt matches, his cheek is the color of green dust. On the square, all the children are waiting to kiss the soldiers, and to be given candy that tastes like soft sweet rubber. Mémé says that all soldiers are devils. They are dirty and smell like smoke, but they are not devils.

When my father puts me down, I run back home. On the way, I spot Lilimoumoute crouching behind the large tree, looking at the American jeeps. He is so afraid that his large mouth is shaking and he can't even grunt. The cigarette butt he has been smoking falls to the ground, so he continues to suck on his fingertip, blowing on it like a cigarette. He is careful to hide from the children or they might throw stones at him. He does not have anything to give them, like the soldiers.

I make sure not to enter the kitchen again until the soldiers our father brought home for breakfast have all left. Later, Mémé is upset at Papa because he made her cook two dozen soft-boiled eggs. She says that no human beings on earth, except barbarians, eat eggs for breakfast.

"They're Attila's Huns, all of them, Germans, American. No difference. If it is not raw flesh, it is eggs they want for breakfast, and then, out they go, bombing, razing cities." Mémé hates the war because the Germans bombed our street and then the English bombed the entire city. She says that Pépé died after the English blew up his old ships in the harbor. Since he was too old to command a ship, like in the Great War, he said he would leave Brest only if they carried him out, feet first. It was Papa who had to carry him onto the truck when we had to leave, and Pépé died of pain because of the bumps on the road and the heat. He asked that I should be placed right next to him. He held my hands in his and said, "Bless you little one," and never spoke another word, Mémé said.

Chapter Eleven

A grey-haired man, his skin dry as a dead tree, comes to visit Mémé. She asks Susie to leave when they come into the room, but she doesn't see me under the dining-room table. When her back is turned I crawl behind a chair and try to make myself very small.

They talk about the war and about Uncle Raymond. The man hands Mémé a broken pair of eyeglasses and says "That's all I could save, Madame, but it was him, I'm certain, on top of... of that pile. Madame, I'm sorry... I made sure he was no longer moving, for they would throw the sick with the dead down that hole. I'm so sorry, Madame. But he did ask me to come to see you... after. Yes, God has spared me, but... if only He could have spared me this." Mémé keeps stroking the broken eyeglasses with the tips of her fingers. Her eyes look away, as if she is counting the books in Pépé's bookcase. Then she just stares at the stuffed red and yellow parrot Pépé brought her back from Africa. Now I see that although the man looks very old, he is actually younger than Papa. When he breathes he makes a strange sound, and soon he bends down and puts his grey head inside both his hands. He whispers, "Madame, Madame, listen to me, listen, your son was a hero. Not only what he did before his arrest but even after, in the mines, before we got transferred to that hell. He sacrificed himself for his comrades time and time again. Madame, your son was a true hero." The grey-haired man's back is shaking, but Mémé does not listen. She looks right through Pépé's bookcase now, as if she has found the dark hole she was looking for, behind it. When the man gets up to leave, she does not let him go. She holds his arm. "Stay, stay. Have a cup of chocolate with us." And the man's body makes strange creaking noises as he walks to the kitchen, with Mémé holding him up.

Chapter Twelve

One winter, Uncle Raymond came to stay with us. After dinner one evening, he took a small machine out of a black case and he pushed every button on it to make perfect words on the paper. But first, he made sure that all the shutters were closed all the way and the curtains drawn, so that no crack of light would show from the outside. He sent me out into the street to check if the house looked pitch dark. The Germans had ordered it, so that the English planes, which we could hear at night sometimes, would not recognize France and liberate it. When I came back inside, uncle Raymond was sitting at his machine; he turned his head to smile at me. "You're a good girl, Vivi. After the war, your Maman can send you to Vichy to visit with us." His eyes were very big, with a golden light in them, just like Maman's. The next morning, he asked Maman to sew little bits of paper inside his coat and Susie told me in secret, because she can't keep a secret, that they were messages for the Resistance fighters hiding in the woods.

Our grandmother forgot to cook the soup the evening the young grey-haired man came to see her and many more evenings after that one. And since Thérèse went back to take care of her sick mother, no one helps in the house anymore. Everything is dirty in the kitchen because Mémé cannot clean the floor and wash the dishes; her legs are so weak, she says, that sometimes she cannot come down the stairs. Susie does not come out of her room, she is so busy trying on dresses or making new ones out of Maman's. No one boils the milk anymore or pulls water out of the well. Papa is in Paris and we have no butter or eggs. Mémé gives coins to Augustine to go buy fish and meat, and she comes back with rotten fish and bones for the soup. The grocer sells yellow leeks and mildewed onions and carrots as soft as sponges. The postmaster's wife, Madame Keiffer, comes to see Mémé and brings her the newspaper and sugar. She has the eyes of an owl and she inspects every corner of the kitchen, telling Mémé, "Really, Madame, your grandchildren should be taught to help. Your Susie could be made to clean up, and Augustine here should wash these dishes." Before she can finish, Augustine has climbed atop a chair and she starts yelling at Madame Keiffer.

"Leave us alone, old witch!" and she runs out of the kitchen. The postmaster's wife gets up to run after Augustine, who now is on the landing, and before she can finish saying, "you drippy-nosed, insolent..." Augustine spits right on her hat. Madame Keiffer runs out of the house now, swearing she'll never set foot in "that filthy barn again." Mémé does not even scold Augustine. She just says, "Good riddance, one less leech in my coffee."

Now Mémé stays in her room almost all morning, sitting in front of the dresser mirror. She looks like someone else lately, not our grandmother. Her hair is all unkempt and she doesn't go in front of Maman's mirror to brush it like she used to, and her face is white. Her eyes don't see. She says that she needs new eyeglasses and so she doesn't wear any. Her eyes look just like Jesus' mother on the stone Calvary in the church square, just two holes made of stone. And her fingers cannot tie the black ribbon around her neck anymore, she trembles so much. Her comb keeps falling out of her hand and I keep picking it up, putting it back in her lap. When I tell her, "Mémé, do your hair up," she mumbles that she has lost her hairpins, which she has not. When she finally combs her hair, bunches of long white strands fall off. She powders her face in the wrong places, like her eyes and mouth. She talks to herself, repeating the same words over and over. "Gone, my children... the last ones, yes... the two last ones, same month, same year. I am cursed. Oh Lord, did you have to put my boy in that hole? And a hole for her, too, my beloved one, my sweet Marie-Madeleine, my little saint. I shall have to put all three of them together, and make the grave bigger. No, no, just a plaque. "

When the priest comes to see her in the kitchen, she shuffles her feet under the table, as if she wanted to run away from him. "No, no. No consolation. I'll never set foot in your church again. No, no, it's all a lie. God does not hear mothers."

Mémé thinks that her son won't ever come back from Germany, from that hell the young grey man talked about. Even though Uncle Raymond is a hero and could do all he wants, even impossible things, like flying away from any hell. Somehow, the grey man, who is not a hero, came back from Germany. Every day I try to tell her that it is time to go to the cemetery, but she does not hear me. One afternoon, at last, she raises herself and puts her black hat on. "Yes, Vivi, let's go talk to her, she needs flowers." Mémé is wearing her bedroom slippers, but I don't tell her because I don't want her to sit down again and never get up. Augustine and Claire are rolling bread dough on the bedroom floor, playing pastry shop. Augustine feeds the filthy dough to Claire, but Mémé doesn't see anything anymore and I am glad she didn't ask them to come. They are still in their nightshirts and I am sure that Mémé would not have noticed the difference, but the butcher and barber standing at the doorsteps of their shops would have guessed that Mémé can't see anymore.

84

I take Mémé's hand in mine to walk to the cemetery and I carry the water pitcher with the other hand. Half way down the street, I realize that we don't have flowers for our tomb. When we go into the cemetery, I see the beautiful blue hydrangeas and I get an idea. I lead Mémé to our tomb and I come right back to the entrance. With all my strength I pull off one branch, and I cut the side of my hand. It burns, but I don't care. I run back and place the branch in the biggest vase we have. I build a wall with large pebbles all around the vase so that the wind won't tip it over. Mémé does not notice the blue hydrangeas. Then, all of a sudden, as she crosses herself, she turns to me, almost smiling, "That's right, Vivi, you'll always find the right extra things at the right time." I know that she says that because she thinks that I am the extra one in the family and even if I could make a whole hydrangea bush grow out of our tomb and bloom forever, she still would not believe that I love her much more than my sisters do, that I love her just like I love

85

Papa. Mémé loves my sisters much more than me, just because they don't love Papa. She says that I am my father's spitting image. I am tall for my age and skinny like Papa, that much is true. I know that I'll never grow fat like Augustine because I don't like cream and butter very much. I like only the heel of the bread, artichokes, and eggs. And I am tall because I run a lot and I climb up trees faster than boys.

When we walk back through the cemetery, I don't skip on the edges of the gravestones. I don't even count the small angels, and I look away, fast, before I can see a crucifix.

We go back every day now, but Mémé takes too long talking to Maman. I say a loud "Amen," and sometimes she crosses herself and stops talking. I walk back with her, holding her hand. She says she will ask the shoemaker to make her a cane. She always wears her bedroom slippers now, because of her bad toes, and I can see that the gravel hurts her feet. I say that we should go to the cobbler's shop for new shoes, but every day she repeats, "It's no use, no use. I don't have much further to go." Mémé does not make sense anymore. In the kitchen, she keeps losing her vegetable knife, or she lets her new eyeglasses fall into the soup. She drops the plate she has been holding or spills the hot water. Now that she has stopped buying the newspaper, the doctor does not come to see her in the afternoon, after his rounds. "Good riddance," I heard her tell the Countess, who now comes almost every day for a cup of coffee and a chat with Mémé, because her son, also, won't come back from Germany. Mémé says, "Poor woman. Nothing, she has nothing, not a soul left. Not even a penny, just good-for-nothing woods and that wreck of a castle." I like the Countess, even though she reminds me of the drawing of the heron in the fable book. Her hats are three times as tall as Mémé's, and she wears a cloud of blue and pink lace crossed over her thin chest. Her shoes are tiny and very white, with rows of pearl buttons. She never takes off her long grey gloves, even to sip her coffee, and she does not open her mouth when she talks because she has no teeth left. When she smiles, she covers her mouth with a pretty handkerchief.

This morning on the street, the doctor told Mémé that the Countess cut herself badly on her chamber pot as it broke under her. She won't come to visit with Mémé for a long while and I shall miss her. If I knew the way, I would go to see her in her woods and crumbling castle, and stay with her a little while.

Mémé scolds me much less now. She keeps asking Susie to do a lot of things, calling her by Maman's name. Susie told me that she is going to run away to Paris to live her own life. Her suitcase is already packed. It's full of dresses, hair curlers and ribbons, and she has exchanged the beautiful star from the top of our Christmas tree for a pair of nylon stockings.

Chapter Thirteen

Papa is leaving again for Paris to see his blind mother and the big parade for the Liberation. The other day, Mémé was furious with him, and she even cried because he made her dress us in our Sunday clothes to go visit a widow who has two sons. They live near the woods, but on the other side of the village. They have three large houses so old that only the middle one still has a roof. "You can't call it a chateau, it's just a rundown manor," Papa quipped as we drove up in his friend's Renault.

One of the boys took my hand in his to show me around. The chapel has beautiful statues, and one is of the Archangel Michael killing the dragon with his sword. There was real blood on it. In the stable, the boy told me that their three horses can beat any champion horse at the races. He also told me that his father is a hero in the war but that he'll never come back. I asked him if his father went to that hell, like Uncle Raymond. "No, straight to Paradise," the boy said. "Heroes always go to Paradise." He is already twelve but he still believes in Paradise. He told me that his mother is the best mother one can have and that he must protect her the best he can. I didn't tell him about my mother being lost, for I wished him to think that I have as good a mother as his. And I could not tell him that I know that Paradise does not exist. I'm sure that if my mother had told me about Paradise, I would have believed her, too, because I thought anything she ever said was true. Now I know that some truths don't always remain true.

The day we spent with the pretty widow and her two sons was the most delightful day I can remember since Maman left us. But as we were leaving, Papa lied to the widow. His friend came to fetch us in his Renault. Papa said, "Oh, here comes my chauffeur," when he saw the car turn around the lawn. The widow, who had been very nice to us, frowned and quickly walked back to her house without saying good-bye. Only rich people can have chauffeurs, and we don't even have a car. We would be poor if it were not for Pépé's Navy pension, which Mémé gives us. Sometimes I don't like Papa at all.

And again yesterday, we had to dress in our Sunday clothes, miss school, and go to Rennes to visit an old spinster and her wrinkly old mother. Mémé didn't cry, but she said she was certain that one of them would turn out to be a witch, "if not the old maid, then, the old lady." And she added, "The old man may have owned a coal mine, but Madame de Kock told me about the doilies she's got stored everywhere, even on the kitchen stove. The old man probably died of doily suffocation, not lung disease. And you, really, Meny, I can't picture you in that doily nest, what with your cigarette ashes dropping everywhere." And she nearly laughed.

What Mémé had said about the doilies all over the place was true. And the old mother was the witch. The old spinster had apparently lost her tongue as she sat staring at us. During the whole entire visit, she kept her hands and knees together, as if she were praying. Augustine and I played tag around the dining-room table and a couple of doilies fell off the armchairs, but we couldn't put them back the right way. We crumpled them up and stuffed them deep inside an empty vase, and the next minute the old mother entered the room. She noticed they were missing and she began looking for them, her eyes nearly spilling out of her head. We ran out just as she was opening her mouth to say, "Where are the doilies?" And, in the next room, we sat close to our father for the rest of the visit so that she wouldn't dare ask us where they were.

Papa is looking hard for a new wife.

I couldn't wait to go back home on the train that evening. I rushed into the compartment and caught my finger in the sliding door. It didn't bleed, but it hurt a lot. Papa brought me a glass of lemonade to make me feel better, and after a while I fell asleep on his lap.

Chapter Fourteen

This morning, Susie told me that my fingertip will stay black forever and that she's happy about it. I know it isn't true, and she says that only because this time she's glad she's not going to be blamed. My blood gushing out of my fingers when she slammed the door on me and my fingertips that won't ever grow back are her fault. I had never heard Maman yell before, but she yelled at Susie when it happened. I heard Mémé talk to the doctor about my fingers. "Madeleine should never have carried a five-year-old in her arms all the way to your house. And barely two weeks before she was due. Running up the street. No wonder the umbilical cord wrapped itself around his neck."

After the doctor left, I asked Mémé what an umbilical cord was. She was angry with me. "You, always listening to what you shouldn't. Go play." Mémé says such strange nonsense when she is with the doctor. If Maman had not carried me in her arms, I would have lost all my blood, I know. So why did Mémé say that she shouldn't have carried me to the doctor's?

Papa was not home the day Maman left us, or I'm sure he would have carried her to the doctor's office as well. Yet, I remember that the doctor and his wife were in Maman's room that evening. Maybe Maman didn't get lost in the woods, maybe she got lost some other way? Mémé is sure that our mother is in Paradise and she talks with her in the cemetery. I think that it is useless, since Maman cannot hear her. Or does she? And did she really tell Mémé she wouldn't be back for a long while, and to put her bed up in the attic?

Our clothes are falling apart. Because they are so old, the washerwoman brings them back half torn to shreds. I saw her slam them against the stone slab at the waterhole. Then, she brushed them with all her might. Picking them up again, she beat them as hard as she could with her wooden bat, as if our clothes were fisherman's overalls, full of dried-up fish scales.

Mémé keeps asking her not to use that brush, but the washerwoman just grumbles, and threatens not to work for us anymore. "It's not that I relish washing refugees' underwear."

So Mémé lets her have it: "That's because you people don't wear any." Mémé's right. Even in winter, I can see her children's bare bottoms when they jump rope in the schoolyard. They aren't the only ones, Augustine says. One day, we saw the farmers' wives come down from their carriages. As the wind flew up their long black skirts, their bottoms looked like pink bread dough.

Any day, none of our clothes will fit anyway. Maman used to make new ones all the time, but there is no one to do it now. Susie brags that she can sew anything, but all she wants is new dresses for herself. At least, on Sundays, she helps us find our white shoes, and she sews our missing buttons. She puts ribbons in our hair and she spits in her handkerchief to clean our chins. Because she likes us to look like pretty dolls when we go to church, she threw Claire's glasses out of the bus window the day we went into town to have our photographs taken. That evening she told Mémé that Claire had lost them. Claire is now three years old but she doesn't know anything, and she squints the same way whether or not she's wearing glasses. I told Mémé the truth, with Susie in the kitchen. After that, Susie stopped lending me her hooded jacket to get the milk at the mill in the evening.

I'm the one who always ends up fetching the milk after school. When it's Augustine's turn, she says she's tired, but she's really afraid of the cows mooing in the dark on the way back. Mémé doesn't dare make her go, or she would blow up and turn all red. When it is Susie's turn and she's sitting comfortably on her bed pillows, chatting and knitting with the grocer's daughter, she promises to sew a coat with a hood if I go. I know that she won't. She is much too lazy and she is a liar. She lies even though she does not have to, just because she likes it.

But I don't mind going for the milk, because I can be alone and think. I have to cross two fields and the brook, then a corner of the woods. In the winter it is so dark sometimes that I can't even see the miller's house, in the meadow just down the hill. The cows are still in the orchard and all I see when I come back are their big wobbly shadows. They moo as if they were calling me, and sometimes it scares me. At other times, their mooing sounds like they are asking me for something. I am sure they want me to take their ropes off their stakes. But I don't dare get too close. Mémé says that cows sometimes kick people, but it is their horns I am most scared of. So I run and spill some of the milk. Other times, it is so peaceful under the trees I stay and sit awhile. I try not to think about crossing the brook, because the rotten, slippery planks the farmer threw over it are a terrible bridge. Several times, I nearly fell in, but I always catch myself.

I like going for the milk. It makes me feel like I could just keep walking and go anywhere I want, and never go back home. It is so big outside under the night sky, and the fields around me are so endless, I could just go on and never turn back around. I would like to get lost on the other side and find Maman there.

Chapter Fifteen

The other evening, I saw a lady coming toward me on the path in the woods. It was almost dark. For a moment, my heart jumped inside my chest and I started to run up to her. I could only think, "Here is Maman, at last." Till she came quite close I felt I knew her. She continued to walk toward me and then I stopped, waiting. Her hair half-covered her face, her mouth was very red, and her eyes shone beautifully in the darkness. I saw that she was not

Maman, for she nearly walked right through me, as if I were invisible. Later, I asked Mémé who the lady in the woods was.

"A mad woman, the Bernardin's mother, cracked all right, poor thing. She abandoned them for the woods after her mare ran away. She keeps looking for it, and she won't find it; her husband sent it to the butcher's."

I remember going to the Bernadin's house, last year, with Maman and Mémé. We all sat at a very large table in a room that looked like the inside of a church. The round ceiling was a very deep red and Maman said it was ox-blood. The servants served us hot chocolate and cakes. When I asked one of the boys where his mother was, he answered "Oh, who knows, who cares, she's probably lost again." Then he started to laugh, a mean little laugh that made me reach out for Maman's hand under the table. Just then, the huge door creaked open. The lady I saw in the woods stood there, not moving at all, as if she did not dare come in. She looked around for a moment, and then left quietly. The Bernardin's grandmother chuckled.

"Here she comes. There she goes." The rows of diamonds all around her black velvet hat shook and tingled and the little boy sitting next to me giggled as if his grandmother had said something funny.

After we left, Mémé told Maman that the children had very good manners, kissing her hand at the door and curtseying, but that just the same, they belonged in the stable with the livestock, since they were raised to be heartless colts by their horse-breeder of a father.

It is odd that the Bernardin children have a mother and they don't care for her at all because she wanders in the woods. And when she opens the door they all laugh and she has to leave again. With us, it is just the opposite. Our mother is really lost and all I ever wish for is that she would open the door one day, and I would make sure that she never leaves us again.

Sometimes, I see Monsieur Bernardin walking up the street, his back as straight as that leather riding crop he carries, his shiny boots creaking and squeaking like a saw that is too dull to cut any wood. He has a black moustache, just like Hitler. Mémé said several times that she hoped they would get him at the Liberation. "That man has no shame, going to lunch with the Germans—a Nazi if I ever saw one."

But they didn't get him at the Liberation. Instead, they got Madame Le Galo, the poor woman who lives in the barn with her five children who don't have any underwear. They said that she had been the enemies' woman and they hung a board full of ugly words around her neck and shaved her head. Then they poured tar all over her and emptied a pillow on her so that she would be covered in feathers, like some thin, giant chicken. The village children followed the laughing crowd of people as she was led to the town hall, where she had to stand in the sun all afternoon. Her children ran behind her. Although they never cried at school even when the teacher beat them, they were crying then. Madame Le Galo didn't cry, and she didn't make a sound. She just stood there, looking straight ahead of her, at nothing. Her beautiful blue eyes stood out like two tiny windows beneath her strange new face, which was like a mask melting slowly under the sun.

I ran back home. I asked Mémé why the Liberation men punished her because of the German friends she had had, and not Monsieur Clément, the mason, who helped the Germans hide mines along all the beaches. Mémé shrugged her thin shoulders. "Don't try to figure it out, Vivi. This is not a good time for justice." I wanted Mémé to explain to me what justice is, but she said that I would have to wait until I reach the age of reason, next year.

I go to school with Monsieur Clément's daughter, and she told some of us that her father is about to build them the biggest house that has ever been built, with three bathrooms and running water. I could not help telling her, "That's good. Then, next year, when it's going to be a better time for justice, your father can wash the tar off his head in his new bathroom." She said that she would have her father tell the Mayor what I had said, and maybe they would put tar all over me. I answered, "And how could they do that to a hero's niece? I didn't plant any mines on the beach, like your father." She yelled back, "Oh, sure. But what about your grandma, that Jew?"

When we went home for lunch, Mémé shrugged her shoulders again and again when I asked her if she is a Jew and what a Jew is. "Eat, eat," is all she said. In the evening, I asked Papa if Mémé is a Jew and what was a Jew.

"A Jew?" he said. "Oh, that. Well, if it had not been for that damn notary who drew up the inventory at the time of your grandpa's death, well..." and he stopped.

"Papa, what is an inventory?" I asked, because I did not want him to stop talking to me about Mémé being a Jew.

"An inventory? It's a long piece of paper, a list of everything I had to bring from Brest under the bombing, and just before your grandfather died. We had to call in the notary, you see, and he had to write everybody's name down, even your grandma's. A Jewish name all right."

"What is a Jewish name?"

"Oh, a name, a German name that ends in 'mann' or something like that. Good thing I was there that day, your mama wouldn't let me lie, she was so afraid of everything. So I wrote down only half of your Mémé's name. I must say it sounded a bit strange, even to that ignoramus of a notary, but not so ignorant after all, the way he came around during the war, pestering your Mémé, wanting to buy your grandfather's books and antiques when I wasn't around. And your grandma gave him whatever he pointed his finger at, that scum."

Now I know what an inventory is, but I still don't know what it is to be a Jew, except that it has to do with having a German name that ends in "mann." Maybe it is not being French. Mémé said her grandmother could not speak a word of French.

"God bless her kind soul. She used to visit us in Nancy during the Great War when I was little like you. Her bags were always full to the brim with food she had prepared, cakes, and those candlesticks of hers. She only knew the word 'eat' in French." I guess it's true that Mémé is Jewish, but that's her secret. The notary guessed it, too.

Hitler hated the Jews, and he made them all prisoners in Germany, Susie told me the other day on the way to the beach. Her first boyfriend's house remained shut this summer and she said, "I reckon they took him, too, in Paris."

"Did they take him to Germany?" I asked. But she pretended not to hear me. I asked her again, and she said, "Maybe to that hell." It is not true, she lied again. Or is that why Papa had to lie to the notary, on the inventory papers? I just wish Papa had lied completely, because I cannot stand the notary's face when he comes to see Mémé, pretending to ask about her health and all the time looking at our grandfather's things in the display cases, and the art on the walls. There should be a place for people like that. All Mémé says about the notary is, "Oh, just another nouveau riche. Another one, thanks to the war. He tricked the poor Countess out of her family's portraits, against a stack of no-good money, and he hung them in his own living room, that son-

107

of-a-pig-dealer. He won't trick me out of one more book."

Now that the war is over, Mémé says that if she could, she would settle a few accounts with the doctor, the notary, the priest and the postmaster, who is also the tax collector. He keeps Mémé's pension check in his drawer for days, and during the war he forced her to pay taxes on it, even though she was not supposed to.

Last evening, as she tucked me in, I asked Mémé again what a Jew is. She said, "Vivi, at times, it's dying of fear. Maybe your Maman died of fear, having to go to church every morning, and inventing sins to confess to that priest. Jews don't die that easily, though. I never went to confession, no, never."

Did Maman die because she was a half-Jew or because she confessed to sins she didn't do to please the Pope?

Maman is not lost in the woods then.

Chapter Sixteen

All the coal Papa brings home is used to heat the stove in the kitchen, and for the small fireplace in Mémé's room. My bed was there too, along with Augustine's and the baby's crib, but Mémé decided I should sleep in Maman's room all by myself. I don't mind being alone, because Augustine is becoming meaner by the day. Yesterday, after she took my favorite doll, and Mémé didn't stop her, she started laughing.

"You don't have a Mama! I do! Mémé doesn't like you, and neither do I." I wonder why she says such nasty things to me. Anyway, I hate the bad smell in Mémé's room in the morning, when the baby has again wet her crib. I like it alone in Maman's room. When I close my eyes before falling asleep, I know she's near me, like before. She's not in Paradise.

Papa is away the whole week for his job. On Sundays, I go up to his room with Susie and Augustine and he reads us stories, or shows us his coin collection. I miss him a lot in the evening. Now that it's cold outside it's even colder in Maman's room. My bed is all the way in the corner, next to the window. Papa gave me one of his blankets. I heard him tell Mémé that he didn't want me to sleep there all alone, without any heat. Mémé got mad, and said she's had it with me, and with three beds in her room! So I told Papa that I like it in Maman's room. When it's very cold I don't take off my clothes and slip under the covers very fast. I found Maman's blue shawl inside the dresser. I stuffed it inside my bed and I wrap my legs in it. No one knows I have it, since I go to bed by myself, and Mémé doesn't even come to kiss me goodnight. In the morning, I don't have to get dressed in the awful cold. I know Maman is right there, at night, like before.

Yesterday, Papa got more angry than I've ever seen him. He put his hand around my arm and then gave Mémé such a look, like the priest when he tells us about Christ dying on the cross because of all the evil in the world. "You don't even feed her properly! Look at her arms!" But it's not Mémé's fault. I eat very little because I hate meat. Susie always helps herself to the vegetables first, and sometimes when it's my turn there's only a spoonful left at the bottom of the pot. But I don't care very much. I don't like to eat a lot, like Augustine who wants to stuff her face all the time. Even the bread tastes like moldy leaves. But sometimes when I lie in bed hungry I'll think about springtime, and climbing over the wall around Madame Le Galo's orchard and filling my belly with juicy cherries.

I heard Papa tell Mémé he's going to take me to Germany with him, as soon as his brother finds him a job with the army. "That's right, good riddance. And it'll be you who kills her!" Sometimes I don't understand the way Mémé thinks at all. Papa would never do anything to hurt me—I am his favorite little girl. He tells me so when my sisters aren't around, but made me promise not to tell.

The war might be over, but it's just like before in the house in the winter; it's dark and very cold and there isn't much food, except when Papa brings home some eggs and butter from the farms. There is no flour at all, the bread is yellow and hard. Mémé warms the milk in the morning before we go to school, and since I'm the one who carries it home from the mill, she lets me have as much as Augustine. Soon, Papa will take me to Germany and I won't be cold anymore.

Chapter Seventeen

Now that it is summer, Susie takes us for long walks down to the beach, just like Maman used to. Every time we pass the blue-shuttered villa, Susie's voice changes completely, because it is her boyfriend's house. She chatters on and on, and if I don't listen, she doesn't care. Her bird-like chirping is better than Mémé scolding me, Augustine's yells, and Claire's cries. My little sister just cries and cries all day long, and squints.

Susie tells me that if Jacques comes this summer she will kiss him for sure, then they'll get married and she'll go to Paris and buy herself lots of clothes at the Bon Marché. I know she means it, but I also know that it won't happen this year. Fourteen-year-old girls don't marry all of a sudden. First, she will have to kiss a lot. She calls it necking and she even

113

knows a song about it. I would hate to have to kiss a boy. Boys are grubby and dirty and their voices sound like angry old women's. Their knees look like muddy stones, and they use them to hold their enemies down the ground.

Susie wheels Claire in her stroller, and Augustine and I share the tricycle, which keeps losing its front wheel. When we can't put it back on, Augustine gives it back to me and says it's my turn. And as soon as Susie fixes it, she starts screaming: "It's my turn!"

It's a long way to the beach. From the top of the road, the sea is no bigger than a glass of water in between the trees. But once we reach the shore it's as vast as the sky. I think some people can do the same trick; they'll shrink to the size of a hazelnut if they don't want to be found.

The hot road stretches under our tired feet. My soles are burning and the road continues to stretch longer and longer, like an elastic band a giant keeps pulling, just to annoy us. And the sea keeps hiding. But when I sit down for a second, the sun stops moving and waits for me.

I look for all the secret signals to make the road shorter. Just after the first big curve is the tiny yellow house with its green shutters, always shut tight. It looks hardly big enough for one person lying on a bed, maybe someone who sleeps all day, a fisherman who goes out to sea at night. I asked Susie who lives in the yellow house, and she told me it wasn't a fisherman. "The man in it just drinks wine all the time and changes wives every year," she answered. There is nothing she does not know about the people in the village. The grocer's daughter tells her everything because her parents know too much, Mémé said. The other day, she scolded Susie for listening to all the gossip.

Down the big curve is the swamp. Just like in the church window, the three horses stand still under a cloud that never changes place, because the swamp always seems to have swallowed the clouds in the sky, and holds them in place. Maman once told us the horses grow wings at sunset and fly up into whichever cloud the swamp is holding for them.

Still further down, on the other side of the road, stands the ugly electrical tower the Germans built. It has a grey iron door and there is a great buzzing noise inside, that makes the door vibrate. It sounds like a snoring dragon.

The poorest children in the entire town live next to the electrical tower, in a huge barn with nothing but one tiny dormer window that can't even be opened because it's too high above the rafters. They have to keep the large door open all the time to get a bit of light inside. Their mother, Madame Le Galo, stands at the door now and her eyes turn into slits, as if the spot of road in front of her stable belonged to her. Her face turns red and she spits on the ground. Susie says "Don't look. She's furious at the world because she never had a husband and never

116

will. She can't even count her children anymore." I don't think Susie is right about Madame Le Galo. I would be mad at the world too if they had shaved my hair and covered me in tar and feathers. I tell her she's sad because her kids are even dirtier than they were before the war, and have to wear the same torn pinafores day in and day out. Susie shrugs.

"Who cares?" She doesn't really care about anything I say since she is wearing her prettiest summer dress, pale blue with white dots, which she made with one of Maman's old ones.

Suddenly, just after we have passed the stable, a rain of cherry pits falls on us. Susie starts running away with Claire's stroller, Augustine gets off the tricycle and starts picking up dry bits of horse dung to throw back. We hear the children's voices from behind the wall of the cherry orchard. Susie calls to Augustine to drop the horse dung, but she won't. I am trying to figure out how I can climb the wall when I feel Susie's hand grabbing me, and she makes Augustine drop her bits of dung.

"Let's get away fast from those devils," she cries, her dark mascara-lined eyes darting towards the shore, wishing she were there already. She is wrong, they are not devils at all. As we escape down the road, I almost tell Susie that I would not mind living like them, except for the cold in the winter and no underwear, stockings or wool sweaters.

They go to school only when they want to. They never have to wash their hands or be polite with the grownups. In the summer they run around barefoot, and it doesn't hurt their feet to climb trees. I'm sure that their mother does not know fairy stories like Papa does, but I would rather have a mother to talk to now that I can read any book I want. Since Papa left to go to Paris, I have no one to talk to in the house.

I want to rest, or else I would like to walk slowly down the tree-lined path that doesn't lead anywhere. We used to sit beneath a big oak tree near the entrance when Maman got tired. And she told us that a kind witch lives inside the hollow trunk. Now Susie says that only mean owls live inside trees, as if she had never heard Maman talk about it. And she won't let us rest our feet, not even for a minute, because she's in a big hurry to meet boys on the beach.

Maude, the meanest girl in my class, lives just off the road in the pink villa behind the tall daisies. She is also a refugee from the city. She never wants to sit next to anyone, because she's too good for the rest of us. Her grandmother holds her hand to walk her to school in the morning, and back home for lunch. Then it's back to school after lunch, and after school she's always waiting for her, in her purple floral hat. Neither one ever nods or says hello to anybody, unless it's the mayor. Maude's shoes are of the shiniest black I have ever seen, with a silver buckle as big as a tea kettle on top. Our shoes are falling apart and they have become colorless. But Mémé

119

still does not want us to wear wooden shoes with fur inside, like the other children. How I long for clogs stuffed with soft rabbit fur! My toes are curling inside Augustine's old shoes, but Mémé says I'm lying when I tell her that my feet are much longer than Augustine's, even though I am younger. Soon, I have to take the shoes off, because the blisters hurt me too much. We march like the soldiers do, to the beat of all the songs we know. One of them goes, "One kilometer on foot, wears out, wears out our soles. One, two… two kilometers on foot …," till we count up to a hundred, at the top of our lungs, our mouths dry, our tongues hurting, and so hot. We finally smell whiffs of warm vanilla from the crêpe stand on the beach. We don't have money to buy any crêpes, or even a cup of lemonade. But we are almost there now, and the road suddenly becomes flat and very wide. The blue sea looks like one of those desert mirages Papa talks about sometimes, too good to be true. I'm afraid it might drain out at any moment. Or else rise, and keep rising, higher than the beach and the road. But it stays in place, doing nothing much, its dazzling blue diamond dimples winking at us, held in place by its immense belly, which stretches all the way to America.

On either side of the road, the fishermen's gardens are hidden under the red and blue fishing nets drying in the sunshine. Large dahlias, yellow, red, purple, push up from below, trying to swing their heads in the wind like us.

Sometimes I hear a long, very long hum in the distance, near the sky. I listen, and I become lighter and lighter. It comes from way across the fields and the swamps, from way above, as if the sun were making some mysterious call, telling all the birds, the horses, the cows, the summer insects marching across the grass, even the fish in the sea and us on the road, to just stop and listen carefully to its song before continuing to walk and float and swim, every day and forever, around and around, like mad specks of dust.

Susie tells me to walk faster; she doesn't know what is soothing, she doesn't hear the faraway hum over the horizon. I tell her, "Listen, listen to the sky; it's singing over there…"

"That's just a hay-thrashing machine, you dumbbell."

I don't want to walk any more. I'm so sweaty and hot, and the beach will be even hotter. I would like to lie under a large shady tree all afternoon and listen to the sky. I would like to go to sleep and dream. But Susie pretends that she doesn't hear me and I know why. One of the boys from the summer camp is going to teach her how to swim. He's as hairy as a bumble bee and smiles at her so that she won't notice. He'll float her at the surface and won't let go of her, which is what she likes the best, not the swimming part. Without him, she'd sink and drown.

I fall asleep on the beach after playing with Augustine, but I don't dream. We made a fairy castle out of sand and seaweed, and dug tunnels and ditches to slow down the tide. I had a lot of fun making each curve appear and disappear under the water's ebb and flow, and we made the tunnels so that the sea would fill them up little by little and then finally carry away the dams and the bridges. Finally, the walls crumbled away as the wavelets crawled up higher and higher. Augustine blamed me, of course.

"It's all your fault if the tide destroyed everything. You could have remembered it was going to come up." She ran after me screaming, "You could have remembered." I splashed her, and then ran into the ocean because Augustine is too afraid to go in past her waistline, although she's so fat she'd definitely float no matter what. Augustine always wants to keep everything forever, even if its ice cream or a castle made with nothing but sand, which can't last anyway.

123

Susie finally gets out of the water with her furry boyfriend and tells Augustine to shut-up and leave me be. I lie down on the warm sand and let the hot sun dry the water on my skin and watch my little goosebumps magically disappear into my skin. I stare at the fisherman's red sails going out to sea, so far away. One day I'll go over the horizon as well. Maybe that is where I can finally find Maman; maybe Heaven is the blue of the sea forever melting into the blue of the sky. After a long time, the red sails seem to stop moving, and yet they reach the invisible line between the sea and the sky, and then disappear. Maybe the ocean stops where the sky comes down on it, or else there is a different ocean out there and it all starts all over again.

At night there is no one on the beach to watch the fishermen come in, and every day at sunrise they go out to sea. They are not even afraid of storms, for if they were, they would never go out at all.

The mushy sand wakes me up. My legs are drenched and my feet have sunk into the sand and so have my calves. I get up as fast as I can and run up the beach to my sisters. Susie isn't there and Augustine makes a funny grimace towards the dunes.

"Look, now that she's finished learning to float, she's over there with the ugliest boy in the world." Then I hear Susie's strange laugh coming from the dunes but I can't see her behind the tall grass. She sounds almost like a goat. Susie is fifteen now, and she can walk upside down on the sand like a spider because she practices her gym every day. I hope I don't ever become like Susie, showing off and standing on my head all day long to make the boys look at me.

Claire is hot in her sand hole and she's crying; she never wants to play near the water with us. Augustine and I decide to fill up Claire's hole with water, at least twenty pails of it, to cool her down

125

and make her stop crying. But the water just disappears at the bottom of the hole.

The next morning, the doctor comes over and says that Claire has a terrible case of sunstroke. Mémé scolds Susie for having forgotten Claire's straw hat. Susie didn't forget it, she simply does not like the hat, and says Claire looks like a sad little crow that fell off the nest when she wears it, for it has black velvet ribbons to tie it and a bunch of fake cherries on top. Susie tells Mémé that she is sick and tired of being a nanny, that she will go and live her own life soon.

"Yes you will, in boarding school!" Mémé answers, hitting her cane on the floor to show Susie how serious she is.

Now Susie helps Mémé like two nannies, because if there is anything Susie hates even more than washing the dishes and taking Claire for walks on her stroller, it's studying.

Chapter Eighteen

It's almost the end of summer, and Papa has not come back from Germany, like he promised. He has a new job with the Occupation Army. Mémé takes us less and less often to the cemetery to pray to Maman. And when we go, all she does is stare at that tomb in the ground, covering it with vases of flowers. But Maman is not there. If I told her that, she would scold me, or call me the extra one. She does not want my help, or else only with the water pitcher and the rotten flowers that we throw on the pile at the entrance of the cemetery. At least she doesn't cry anymore, and she has started wearing her mauve hat again. Her new shoes have American plastic soles as thick as two slices of bread. And she can even walk around without having to hold on to anyone, because the carpenter made a nice new cane for her from a piece of cherry tree.

Mémé has put a very ugly marble book on our tombstone, with a small French flag in one corner. Carved on the page in gold letters are the dates "March 6, 1944, Pleuven" and "March 14, 1944, Dachau, Germany." Mémé has lost her daughter, her son, and her husband because of the war. She is alone now with the four of us.

Papa's cousin came to get him as soon as he returned from Germany. They went to the Café, and he said "Come-on Vivi, come and keep us company." Maybe he didn't want to be alone with his cousin.

"You're a widower and you better do something about it," she said soon after we got to the café, talking loudly so that everyone could hear. "The old lady won't last much longer. And you know very well that no one will have you here. To your good luck!" She smiled as she raised her glass of wine. In the café, all the men's heads turned toward our table. Some of them grunted and nodded as if they knew that too. Even though I don't like Papa's cousin, I think that she was right about Papa's bad luck here, for I saw the pretty farmer lady whose brothers threatened to chop him up if he ever set foot at their farmhouse again. I didn't want to get off the bike that time, and I asked Papa to please go back home, fast.

Later I heard Mémé talking about it. "How could you? A farm girl!" And I saw the nice widow with two sons that Papa tried to trick about us being rich and having our own chauffeur, and the old spinster who could only sit and pray because of her evil mother, who smothered her husband with her doilies.

Papa promises again to take me with him next time he goes to Germany, when we go to the train station to say good-bye. But I don't miss Papa a whole lot anymore when he goes away. He said he would be back with a suitcase full of toys but I don't play with toys much anymore, since Augustine always ends up breaking them or saying they are hers.

Papa never went looking for Maman and now he's forgotten her. One day, the doctor's wife came for Mémé because Papa had some important news. So we all went to the doctor's house and we waited for the telephone in the office to ring. Susie picked up every magazine she could find and her eyes became huge like saucers looking at all the pictures of pretty ladies in pantyhose and skirts, like the ones the tourists wear in the summer to show off their calves. I could guess that she was thinking about how to cut up every last one of Maman's dresses to make them like the ones in *Elle*. When the telephone rang, Mémé listened to Papa for a little while and didn't say anything until the end. "Don't bother," she told him finally, "if what you bring home is another curse on your children. Keep her there." Then she put the phone down very hard. She meant our new mother, who is in Germany with Papa.

Chapter Nineteen

When I think about Maman, now, it's not the same. Last month it was my birthday and Mémé told me that, soon, I shall reach the age of reason. And instead of a toy, she gave me two secrets. The first one is that even though I am the extra one, I am also a lucky child, and to prove it to me, she now sends me every week to pick up her lottery ticket. She gets a refund each time, and once she even won 300 francs. But it is her second secret I like the most. Mémé told me that Maman once said to her that "Vivi will always fall back on her feet, no matter how bad things are." When I was a baby, I got sick after being fed the wrong milk in the bomb shelter, but I got well again. My fingers won't grow back, but they don't look as ugly as before. And my stomach healed after I ate all the rotten baptism candies.

Sometimes it feels as if Maman knew that of all her children, I was the one who would never give up thinking about her, remembering her, every day of my life. And that as long as I remember her, the world will never stop growing, and I'll discover beautiful things and wonderful secrets. For Maman is everywhere, I know that. She never sleeps anymore, and she always sees me. At times, it feels as if she is inside me, so that even though I look small and am only six years old, I am really almost a grown up.

Last year, when Maman was still with us, I didn't truly know it. I could see her all the time, but I would not really look at her. I don't remember Maman's face too well. Now that she's gone forever, it's as if Maman and myself are one. She let me be born through her, alive, not like our baby brother.

She taught me everything I know, and she never called me "the extra one."

I know that Maman is dead. Just like they said, she died of blood-loss and fear, because it was nighttime and there was nobody to take her to the hospital. She won't come back to our house, ever. But she is not in a sky-paradise, which does not exist, or in the cemetery.

She lives inside me and will remain there until I die. And I'll make sure she doesn't die again. I'll make her well and happy. And when I grow very old like Mémé, we'll vanish together, like two waves melting quietly on the sand.

The End